E
BER

Berson, Harold

A moose is not a
mouse

A MOOSE IS NOT A MOUSE

A MOOSE IS NOT A MOUSE *by Harold Berson*

CROWN PUBLISHERS, INC., NEW YORK

ALSO BY HAROLD BERSON

The Boy, The Baker, The Miller and More
Henry Possum
Balarin's Goat
How the Devil Gets His Due

Manufactured in the United States of America
Library of Congress Catalog Card Number: 74-16552
Published simultaneously in Canada
by General Publishing Company Limited
First Edition

The text of this book is set in 18 pt. Bembo.
The illustrations are 4/color pre-separated ink & wash drawings
with wash overlays reproduced in halftone.

A MOOSE IS NOT A MOUSE

Victor was a city mouse. He had spent
all of his life living in an apartment
building. On sunny days, Victor liked
to go on the roof and admire the skyline
of the city. But his mother always said:
"Watch out for the cat!

"He sleeps with one eye open and you
can't hear him when he walks about
looking for mice on his soft, padded paws."

On rainy days, Victor liked to curl up
with a good book. He read about

field mice,

and kangaroo mice,

mice who lived in the desert,

and mice who lived in the forest.

He even read about knights in
armor on horseback and he dreamt
of being a mighty knight

who conquered the cat.

Victor often listened to his older brothers
and sisters and his Uncle Jack read from
the encyclopedia. Uncle Jack lived in the foreign
language department of the library and he was very smart.
Victor tried very hard to understand everything Uncle Jack
read, but sometimes he would get mixed up.

"Was it," he wondered, "the sow,

or

the cow that had horns?

"Was it the cow that went oink oink
and rolled in the mud,

or

was it the sow that nibbled on
grass in the meadow?"

One night Victor heard his Uncle Jack
reading about a moose. "What a strange
way to pronounce mouse," thought Victor.

"Up to nine feet in length and seven and
a half feet high," read Uncle Jack.

"It moves through the northern forests
and has antlers on its head."

"What a strong relative," thought Victor.
"A horned giant. Why can't I be like him?

I can!"

Victor walked over to the sleeping cat.

He yanked his whiskers

and nipped him on the tail.

The cat was surprised.

Then he got angry.

"Why, you are nothing but a mouse. I'll show you what cats do to mice!"

The cat ran! Victor ran faster!
He scurried into a mousehole and
into his mother's arms.

"What did I tell you about the cat?"
she scolded.

"I know," said Victor. "But some day
I will be the size of a moose, nine
feet long and very, very strong, and I
will get that cat!"

"A moose!" laughed Victor's mother.
"You will never be a moose.
A moose is not a mouse.
This is a moose," she said,
as she pointed to a picture in a book.

"But don't worry. You will grow up
to be a strong and brave mouse. You
were the victor, Victor."

And she kissed him goodnight.